Hell's Press Presents

ISBN   978-1-7381321-4-0   (paperback)
ISBN   978-1-7381322-3-2   (ebook)

hellspress.com

Fairie Tales

Momotaro

COUNT FATHOM

Dedicated to...

... you, wandering the path without a compass. striving for the light ,but knowing only darkness. straining to go forward, but seeming to move back. Straight and narrow is the way, and yet it feels so long.

Simplicity, compassion, and the patience of a Saint. Philosophy is sacred, yet she's treated off hand quaint. Realize you have enough, then you are truly rich. Yet jealousy and envy are revealed by facial twitch. Somehow doing nothing, yet leaves nothing good undone. The more you know, no need to show, the less you understand. This thought bestow: the way is slow, you're crawling on your hands. If all you will be given , then the all you must let go.

Eyes can't see the truth if they are covered with debris. Sweep away the clutter if you hope to live life free.

Inspired by Lao Zi

TABLE OF CONTENTS

———✦✦✦———

Preface

Truth and reason are not much in season in the halls of our lords and kings. High above all, they are holding a ball, but only for those that have wings. Gold plated they are, magnificent stars when seen from afar, but all too aware of the lightness of air and just how dangerous would be the fall.

There are few that know what to do, where to go to soften the cage that we're in. Placate the state and patiently wait til conditions create the chance to throw weight and loosen the ruler's linchpin. Others will say, though his morals are grey, this leader is similar in every which way to the last and

the next and it's best to look after your skin.
Don't fight, let them win.

I don't agree. A leadership beastly
and selfish and cruel must be abolished,
no matter the tool, replaced though he be
with just such a fool as to continue the rule
of false reform. A guise often used, when
power's abused, to weather a political storm.
Time he's then given to further deform the
slightest of freedoms we hold. Time patters
on and he'll continue the con, til the leader
again will grow bold. We'll soon settle down
in a habitual frown and obediently do as
we're told.

Momotaro

Mei Ji

Wild and free the wind blows, but not so free as Mei Ji, so the fellows used to say of her. The fierce swirls of her youth compounded into a hurricane, leaving her penniless, barren and prematurely aged. Mei Ji sought help from the wise monks in the mountain. Mounted ignobly on an ass, Mei Ji would spend three seasons traveling 1900 leagues into the godly city in the sky in search of some magic to alleviate the tragedy of her predicament.[i]

Many are the stories of Mei Ji along the path to her destination, and you will hear tell of them in time. But we are eager to relate later consequences of this odyssey and will not be delayed.

The monks received Mei Ji coldly, yet with the grace of an enlightened hospitality. Those monks in the godly city in the sky will surprise you. They agreed to supply Mei Ji with all she desired. After one night, in a cold, barren cell available to visitors, Mei Ji was summoned before the break of dawn. Under a cold cloudless starry terror, she was led to the precipice of a grave decision.

Mei Ji was quite unaware as to the gravity of her choice. Mei Ji approached a ledge upon which several monks stoically awaited, having brought her ass, loaded and prepared to depart. Mei Ji was presented with a peach on a tray. Without further ceremony, as I believe was the intent of the monks after all, to be done with Mei Ji as soon as possible, for something wicked in her nature disturbed them, Mei Ji tore open the peach and devoured it.

Thus she departed on her ass, thrilled at her success. Dawn burst upon Mei Ji and her heart responded. For another three seasons, she rode her trusty ass down from the golden city in the sky. Each step rejuvenated our blackened heroine in spirit and, in fact, in body. The peach, some say, was watered from the elixir of life, the fountain of youth if you will, restoring one to a previous age. Within nine months Mei Ji regressed twenty years, regaining much in vivacity and appeal,

yet retaining the wisdom she had so pain-
fully, shamefully acquired. Almost her most
welcome surprise.

Mei Ji bore child along the journey
down. Mere days before reaching her village,
the child came.

————— ⁺⁺✦✦✦⁺⁺ —————

"A miracle!" proclaimed some.
"Naughty, little monks..." was heard too, in
a whisper. Then giggling. Considered themselves lucky if they weren't stoned to death at
some point by their oh so puritan brethren.
Such is the sad state of man.

The child came. Mei Ji continued in
her old ways for a few more years to build a
little capital. With the return of her youth,
but the retention of her wisdom, Mei Ji cap-

italized her appeal. She moved with infant Momo from one luxurious apartment in one district, to another in another and another after that. This time she wasn't such a drunken slut, and socked away a fair sum before Momotaro was five years old. Yes, that's his name. MeiJi and others called him Momo.

Some assholes called him peach boy. They taunted and teased him, chanting the name over and over. That was a really bad idea, as it turns out. Momo was a relaxed and calm child. He didn't rise easily to taunts and jeers. He lived in a realm above the petty insults and slight torments of lesser creatures. But enough is enough. Two boys together got in Momo's face and chanted peach boy a half dozen times before Momo stood like Jesus on the cross, swung his arms

together with all the power his little kinder-
garten chest could muster and coconutted
those two boys' heads. The legend begins.

MeiJi sadly departs centre stage of our
tale. We're making way for our hero, the
unconquerable, the incomparable, the son
of a whore, Momotaro. From ignoble births
come great things. Plant a seed in cow dung
and watch the mighty oak live centuries of
principled virtue.

Momo

What? No! She's not dead. Not for a
long time. MeiJi is my baby. She's sticking
around. She'll still figure heavily in the pages
to come. Stop jumping to conclusions. You
could never guess anyway. Yes, I'm totally
attracted to MeiJi. But not the dirty part.

I don't like that. But it could be forgiven.
Her tale is not yet told. Not even the dirty
bits. She traded in all the wealth she had
acquired and bought a double plot lot at
a crossroads between the manufacturing
district and two neighbourhoods. MeiJi's
was Mamasan at an upscale brothel dripping
in understated good taste, for MeiJi has an
eye for the beautiful. Exploit away, MeiJi,
for you are free. Be nice to the girls though.
And she was. Have no fear about that. But
sometimes these little bitches need a slap,
and MeiJi wasn't above anything of the sort,
when called for, in her opinion. Meiji was an
enlightened spirit.

Her brothel was well disguised as a
tasteful, expensive evening entertainment
venue, with soft music and slippery ser-

vice accompanied by a small dining area, especially busy at lunch with the executive personnel from the manufacturing district. On the second plot that backed this property was a guarded complex for MeiJi's home, where Momo grew up, and one or two other surprises. No. Not now. Down boy. Stop. Okay. Just one little thing, for now...

Momo was five when the properties where purchased. There were existing building infrastructure on the lot, some of which was scraped immediately. But walls here and there were salvaged. And something was uncovered. But we'll talk about that later. I told you. Just this one thing about the property and Momo, who found a dull blade among the various farm and machine implements

on the yet unrenovated property, in one of
the adjacent sheds.

Are you wondering how even a frugal,
high end escort like MeiJi could squirrel
away enough for not one but two lots of
prime real estate, just begging for development in just five years? Or maybe you
weren't. You'll want to know anyway. Early
in the development of this frontier settle-
ment, a woman was caught and hung in
secret. Her story is a sad one. You'll see
later. The body was buried on what would
one day become MeiJi's plot, and a wicked
sapling burst forth from the very coffin.
Decades later this malicious twisted tree
had poisoned the land. One developer after
another was thwarted, as their foundation
would rot, termites would devour the wood,

plagued by unsolvable moisture issues, every attempt was foiled. The meagre structures MeiJi inherited smelt of failure and decay.

On a visit to the property before her purchase Momo had wandered off. This was a momentous occasion for multiple reasons. Though she didn't know it at the time, this would be last time in her life that MeiJi would whore herself out, an accomplishment and a farewell she would remember well in later years, not for the performance, for that agent was not memorable in any way. Oh! Don't be sad, dear, you were just fine. It's just that I remember the occasion for different reasons. It was a landmark moment in my life.

The agent had eyed her on day one, and she knew it too. He thirsted and she cooled him off. She bargained over the deal with her sexuality and won handsome rewards, learning all the weaknesses of the sellers without ever consummating her promises to the agent. He was led to believe that he would be satisfied when the deal closed.

She learned of the poisoned land and the cursed fruitless tree. Her curiosity piqued, her spirit challenged, her ambition unrelenting, she went to see, to have a peek, a little look. Nothing seemed much out of order. MeiJi was quite surprised, and pleased. Even upon seeing the tree, MeiJi was absolutely certain she could invest in this location with confidence. While MeiJi and the agent were out on one of their long walks about the property, Momo found that dull knife in the shed.

And he found that tree. Momo started in aggressively with that ridiculously dull knife that would squish a block of cheese, and be difficult to do at that. Momo was undaunted. Momo was focused and determined. And Momo made way. Not just through the trunk horizontally, but eventually down into the core, hollowing out the entire root structure at not yet maybe a full five years old? No. Yes. I'm sure. He was fully five at that time. My fault. I had to look back a moment. I apologize.

There's an elephant in the room. Of course! We haven't even mentioned it yet and that's the whole point we were trying to clear up from the beginning. Was Momo a magical creature, inseminated by a peach from the garden of the godly monks high in the heavens? Otherwise, this incident with the hollowing out of the tree has no context, and you'd think it totally impossible, which it was, just that Momo is the god loved son of a peach.

Enraged Momo, with aggression inspired by the gods, attacked the very root of that tree, into the coffin of the sad story witch, and drew forth a medallion, among other trinkets, which was from thence and forevermore hung about his neck.

The contract for the property was consummated that very day. The domain over which MeiJi was to become master was born.

MAMASAN

But back to what we were saying about MeiJi the Mamasan. Her authority was unquestioned by staff and patrons alike. She ruled as queen, with a sharp look, a sharp tongue, and the vengeance of the gods. She even had a dungeon of sorts hollowed into the foundation, rarely but not never needed, to cool off the unruly or punish the wilfully wicked. It wasn't long before MeiJi no longer needed big fellas to pound on the badly behaved. Momotaro was a fully grown man by the time he was eleven years old. He caused no end of havoc in the preceding years, having to be chained up more than once. In fact the dungeon was mockingly alluded to as Momo's play room. More on the chronicles of Momotaro later, as you need to fill in the main lines before you can appreciate the details.

No need to fear. Momo was monstrously huge, but he remained relaxed and calm throughout his life. His adorers bless him as contemplative, meditative, possessing a mental gravity that centres his mind, while ours constantly spin. His detractors prefer to obsess over his volcanic rage. Most who ever knew or met Momo would claim truthfully that they never saw him hurt a fly, going out of his way to not do so on occasion. But there were episodes. Not funny, like when you see am emotional woman throwing a fit in the street. Fearful. Totally unhinged in a hurricane. And we'll see one of those times soon enough.

Momo held fast to an ephemeral moral code all his own. He would not voice any principles of this code, but it existed, and when it was crossed, Momo would focus his will to right the wrong. Though it might not be a wrong you or I might perceive, as Momo was unique in his perceptions. Momo did, occasionally, demand recompense or acknowledgement or apology from unsuspecting persons. One such fellow, refusing to apologize for the insult he had directed at a young lady of the establishment, was crippled for life when Momo broke his leg like a green branch with a twist of his wrist, the leg held fast between thumb and forefinger. The man was resolute that he had not insulted the lady, and the lady herself was not pressing any claim. Momo would not relent. Nor did he when another man stood chattering in front of the doorway, creating a jam of bodies. The man was picked right up off his feet and tossed out the open window from the second floor, luckily landing softly in some shrubbery and suffering no more than minor lacerations and a bruised hip bone from which he fully recovered by the way. Many there are and varied the vignettes painted of Momotaro and his exploits, but let us not deviate, for we should be disciplined.

These moments of violence, including the two described above, were not executed with a thundering lunatic hate, mind you. Momo was mindful, most of the time, and was not easy to rile, but when the code was crossed, action he would take. Momo would say he was impartial if he cared to speak at all. Momo was a man of few words, and those few were not wasted defending himself from the accusations of others. It was received as sacramental fact that Momo was in the right in all his moral judgments. Who would dare oppose him?

Not that you would find Momo daily dispensing his own special brand of justice, a vigilant vigilante. Momo allowed the fabric of time to weave about him, as if he alone were unmoving and unchangeable. He was a spider at the centre of his web, feeling the tug of the strings, their vibrations and harmonies, so fully engrossed in the experience of the moment that he rarely focused on any one incident.

But his detractors were not wrong. A plague had set about the land, and stories of the piling bodies of the dead came from cities far away. Then, quickly, very close. An evil pestilence, an agonizing death, always fatal. But one town removed reported a death by plague, signs on the corpse being unmistakable. Momo left in the dead of night and no news reached home of him, or anything else for that matter, for a fortnite. Momo had massacred the entire town, burnt the corpses, and quarantined himself before returning. Though everyone knew, no one ever mentioned this incident, and Momo therefore was ashamed of all mankind.

The meat of our narrative is fast approaching. A carousel of characters arrive and depart nightly at Orchid, ...

What's that? What does Momo look like? What's he wearing? You want more about Momo as a man before we continue? I suppose it's not out of place. But how impertinent of you! Telling me my duty, you're lucky you get anything at all. And yes, MeiJi's palace, the slut farm, is called Orchid. And what does Momo look like? He's a big dude. A big Japanese dude. What? Yes. Japanese. You didn't know that, you ignorant pleb. Momotaro, the peach boy, is Japanese. And he's awesome. But that's only as you'd expect.

ALGARTH

A carousel of characters arrive and depart nightly at Orchid, and one might not notice a customer in the crowd. An unusual customer. He wasn't there for the girls. Or the boys. He sat alone and nursed a drink for an hour or so and then left, one night after another. Do you think he's some kind of weird psycho? I'm not sure yet myself. Momotaro was aware, but said nothing. The man glanced Momo's way on occasion, but so did everyone. Momo didn't disappear in a room. He was a powerful magnet for attention.

This lank, unkempt fellow with a messy long, but still coloured, beard hanging off his messy long face deserves our respect too. "I am Algarth Oni, and I have a valid claim on property wrongfully taken from me that now resides within the walls of this establishment. I do not claim that wrongdoing has been done by those in possession of my property. Nonetheless, it is rightfully mine. It hangs now round the neck of this Giant I have heard called Momotaro."

A waitress buzzed round our new friend while he was making his fine speech, and he accidentally bumped a table and shook a drink. Momotaro thumped the mallet of his fist on the table nearest, and plates jumped on every table in the room. After a yelp or two, silence reigned, and attention was directed between Momo and our man, Algarth. Algarth repeated his fine speech with a proud tone, yet remaining respectful. Algarth wasn't fooling around, but all could see the beads of sweat begin to break across his slightly wrinkled whispy forehead. All awaited Momo.

Momo said nothing. All was still. Algarth took the two steps unconfident, but determined, towards Momo, "I'll have my family heirloom." Before he knew it, Algarth's entire head was engulfed in Momo's giant paw, and the head was bounced like a coconut off the table nearest, once again suffering unwarranted abuse. Clearly the direct approach was not possible under present circumstances. As Algarth recovered, seated now next to Momo, dishes and glasses were rearranged hastily and without much comment. An tense astonishment sharpened the air. Don't ignore that tension. That's real. That's magic. Anything can happen in such moments, as our antennae are set to receive. What are we capable of?

Momo felt like a puppet master in these moments, comfortably applying the code as circumstances demanded, never experiencing the crippling hesitations of self doubt or fear, and he found that his slightest application of will could order the group, and they would not resist. Nevertheless, Algarth did not relinquish his claim. Looking hard into the eyes of Momotaro, Algarth began, "That medallion around your neck is of incomparable value to me, and, as you'll hear, for many others. It was crafted millennia ago. It's rich in impossible metals, yes, but it has much further value than its mere worth in coin.

"My home is an island at a critical stronghold in the sea, called Onigashima. We were a reliable and trusted trading port, where vessels from all over could resupply, and hold over in a storm. We have been thus since time immemorial. We have a rich local culture, and traditions all our own. That medallion around your neck was a ritual amulet relied upon by hundreds, by our whole community for good fortune, though we knew it not. We simply fared well in trade and lived lives of comfort, attributing success to ourselves and our profound abilities. We were mistaken."

"Two generations back, my very Grandmother was a local apothecary of sorts. Some people thought her mad. The rumours are true, that in my family, the Oni, madness has a foothold. But hers was a gentle madness, and she was accepted as an somewhat eccentric old witch at the fringe of social gatherings. Respect for my family, however, and toleration of our flaws is traditional on the island, as our family bore that amulet as an heirloom. On the solstices, some would pay tribute in a ceremony to the good fortune brought to the island by this very object. It was ancient, and we were the most ancient family known in the land. Not all people followed these traditions, but some still did. Then an horrible tragedy occurred."

"My Grandmother died. The possession of the amulet fell to my mother. Now I must reveal to you an painful fact. My dear mother was most certainly mad. And not in the funny way. She set fire to a man's garden with a potion that blackened the earth around his home to this very day. She wasn't often so violent. She might cackle after securing a glass to a wall with permanent adhesive. Or howl merrily when a bird dropped his business on a man in a park or beach. Harmless enough to be let go about her business in public, but an unholy terror at times. Still she was my mother, and she loved me. My mother bore that magic amulet round her neck as she was hunted by village henchmen all the way out here to the borderlands of our province. She was hanged and buried here, on this very land."

I gotta say, the crowd was into it! They liked this story. They were hooked.

"The death of my dear mother was a blow to me." Here Algarth, paused and allowed some seedling empathy a little air. "I am forced to accept the official account of her death, that my mother hanged herself. The law was not on my side that day. I will cower in endless sorrow, weeping for the justice my mother never received. I have tried my best." Algarth is not a bad guy, it seems, and so thought many, especially one particular girl staff, who was rubbing her hand between her legs rhythmically to the speech. She was a queer one, and this wasn't her first time, most people liked it. Algarth continued un effected.

"Many consider the medallion the seed of our good fortune as a people. My land has withered since its disappearance. The vengeance of the gods is a fearful terror. Storms have ravaged our shores. What little crops we maintained were destroyed, not once but thrice in the ensuing years. Our ports were torn to splinters, and structures built close to the sea were severely damaged, which is to say all of them on the island. Ships could no longer dock, and we lost all our trade, and with it the last vestiges of hope. Here I stand, nearly naked, before you, beseeching on behalf of an entire people for the return of my ancestral property. I have a rightful claim. My mother's amulet, to you, is a mere decoration. My family heirloom is your vain adornment."

Momo abstains from the interactivity that was expected of him. Algarth has little choice but to continue in some fashion or other. The crowd was getting antsy.

"I have been to this land many times before. Long before it was ever disturbed by your development. And I have seen the tree that grew upon her grave. I have wept for her on these very grounds. And I, too, attempted to dig out the roots of that tree and recover my family's medallion, only to fail miserably. And I was not the first to try. "

"Were you here about a decade ago? I think we met, when this place was a small pickle farm for about a year there. We talked about getting those coke furnaces hot to smelt steel, do you recall?." One of the managerial class piped up. Bob. All look his way, and, for the first time, we hear Momotaro speak... He raises his giant limb, from his seated position points a sausage at the man at the full length of that rock smashing arm and says..

"Bob!", with such command, that Bob was ready to self sacrifice. "Shut your mouth." Momo oozes Zeus's authority.

Bob was a regular with both the executive lunch and evening crowd, that horny little bastard maker. Well liked by all, but his wife and kids. Bob sat down, quite ashamed, realizing the inappropriateness of his remark. What an horrible social blunder. Bob shrunk into the shadows in his plush forest green velvet flared highback recliner. Bob was disgusted with himself, and all were disgusted with Bob. He was sure he could buckle down and swallow the shame, with some gentle work he was sure he would recover, with little but an ancient scar. Momo would not forget though.

"I came again, as you have seen, three days ago. I was astonished. The tree has been uprooted. My mother's soul has been released, that is how I interpret this omen. May she find peace in the afterlife that was not afforded her in the flesh. "

"And I find my family heirloom adorning a monster. I have tried and I have failed to recover my property by force. I am now appealing to your own sense of justice, Momotaro. For the entire population of my island, 347 souls, rely upon your right judgment, Momotaro. And if this is not enough, if I have not persuaded you with the justice of my cause, then let me involve your self interest. I have a will, recognized by the court, who at this very moment uphold my claim upon my birthright, the medallion that is your decoration, Momotaro."

Algarth held peace for a moment. Momo ate a banana while Algarth delivered his fine speech. Now he was finished and politely folded the peel and lay it on the much abused table nearest. As Momotaro remained silent, as was his custom, conjectures and opinions began sporadically, and spread virulently. Algarth in has knatty pants, and long suffering leather long coat, his tangled face hair and his unwashed face has biased you towards him. You think him a lout. How could you? Your disrespect is the manifestation of a meagre, deformed spirit.

Momotaro held no such biases. "I will come to your island.", delivered like a smith's hammer on the anvil of death.

"You are a man of honour, Momota-ro. I leave you on your noble word." And at that our mysterious visitor from a far flung land pirouettes his leather long coat, tilts his head and measures a march to the door, and the handle, and oh god!, and he's gone, with great relief.

No more was heard of Algarth. And no more was heard from Momotaro. A half moon's wane and Momo had prepared a pack of comforts for his odyssey. He was off at the pitch of dawn, to walk the leagues of country into the den of the devil she witch cult, Oni. Madmen!

ODYSSEY

Less than half a day march from
Orchid, and we'll skip the fare thee wells
and such from his home, bursting from the
corn field comes an Haokkaido Inu. The
Inu bounds to block the path, skids to a
stop and addresses Momo with soulful howl.
"Yes," said Momo, "I am Hoki" said the
dog, and the bond was set between the two.

Time on the road is long. Between
Momo and Hoki was a shared honour that
neither would sacrifice on pain of death,
a relationship Momo had not felt before.
Hoki was a brother. Hoki had heard of the
Oni. The island of Onigashima had been
cursed these years passed. Rumour told of
lost treasure, a ritual amulet that brought

good fortune to the island and its people. Momo shared the secret of his medallion, and the purpose of his trek, which wasn't entirely clear. Momo would remain above frustration. He would watch and he would listen.

Hoki warned against Onigashima. The people there are desperate, scratching bark off trees to sate biting hungers. Hoki heard tell of horrible bandits, highwaymen, and robbers. Not that Momo would meet a match, but there is nothing to gain. Momo reminded his friend of the pledge he had made before all, and he would not be dissuaded by the horror stories of a hound, even noble Hoki.

Onward they trod, through days of rain and howling winds, finding what sleep they could under a black dome of cloud, rising each morn covered in a chill frost. South was their route, and days folded into weeks. The cold subsided, and their journey staved off the onset of winter for a time. Arriving on the coast of a vast sea, Momo faced out to the void with such stillness of spirit as to blend into the harmony of heavens and earth. Other men may be seen at great distance amidst a messy muddled landscape. Momo was masked in the most naked environment.

Momotaro waits. He is patience personified. A statue facing the sea, through wind and rain, as the heavens roll from night to day, and slowly the seasons give way. The brisk chill of early winter bares the branches while Momo still waits, disguised as he was as one with the land, when along rows a ferry boat up to the shore. The Ferryman lashes a rope to a post and steps with ginger swift caution from the tilting gunwale, but one step from giant Momotaro, whom he had not yet seen.

The ferrymen steps. He is startled. Aghast! His neck snaps sharply back, throwing the hood from about his head, and what a ferryman have we here! He's a monk! Having stepped on the foot of a moster unseen has shocked our friend, and he stumbles back into the water, wet to the knee, and cowering in fear. At first. As Momo gazes down on the Ferryman, his look is not of malice or deceit or devilry of all sort. This monster is perhaps of a principled cast thinks the ferry man, much less distressed.

"Pardon my alarm, friend. I am an excellent judge of character, as a ferryman needs be, and you have, sir, a noble bearing. I would risk to trouble you for a moment of your time."

"Let us sit. Monk. You look like a monkey." Hoki, following faithfully, sat watchfully from the shade of near bark.

"Not the first or last time such an observation will be made. I am an hairy faced man. Mister Master Mumphrey Moriarty Morris Milthrope Macteur is my name. Just Morris, if you please. That the wonder of you went unseen is a worry to an old monk ferryman such as myself. I question my own senses, for you were not there, or not distinct as such. I have grown old and weak, as has the land. We were once young and well together. Travellers from all ports stopped about this sea, and trade flourished. The land paths were worn deep with the traffic of persons and goods, all in commerce and trade throughout the valleys and vales and glades and glens and ferns and fens of the forest, and village market squares filled with all the world's wares, the gowns in the towns and the balls and the halls and the belles and their swells swept through with coin spread sundry in their wake. When a curse struck the land, and we knew not why. Pronounced in the sky that our island would die, we have struggled through many lean years. The crops will not grow, though we still hope and sow, and spend night after night wet with tears."

Sat now, along the shore, our three friends share in the air of innocence, found rarely among men. As the wise rhesus regaled in past glory, then the plummet from heaven's gate into the painful depths of misery and loss, Momo sat passive, permissive, and as always patient, awaiting fate's flame to flicker.

"Take us to Onigashima."

"A rare fare, my friend, I'm pleased to be of service. I will deliver you to the island for your coin, but under no condition will I disembark from the ferry. Onigashima is cursed. For once was an amulet, blessed with the light, that brought luck to the land and her people."

Pushed off from the shore, the ferry rocked gently to the ferryman's chore. The waves lapped intently, unceasing, but gentle against the wood of the hull.

"There is an family on the island, the Oni, an ancient clan. Some say they are primordial. Back to the garden of the first men. I cannot elaborate on this claim, but the Oni have long hosted their ritual traditions. Their creed they spread about the land, and admittedly the land has thrived under their management. Many have made their fortune while the Oni reigned."

Hoki settled to the floor of the ferry, having been alert and unsure for some time.

"In recent times the Oni have lost much of their sway in the villages. Here and there, people still adhere to the principles of their past. But a mostly secular, elected officialdom has come to manage most of the island affairs for generations. Some time ago now, I struggle to say when, an Oni mother, a mad witch, was hunted from the land, died, and the amulet was lost, as were the fortunes of the island and its people."

Morris sighed, paused, and sat, as the sun shone speckled through covers of cloud, then continued with his chat.

"The wind whispers to me, and I listen. I am an humble source and warn you to believe me, but the hunt of that woman was more than a murder. The officials conspired to eliminate the Oni from their position, even if only ceremonial, in society."

Morris oared out into the ocean once more, his vigour restored, certain that truth revealed is an healing and goodness unto itself.

Momo unbuttoned from the neck and drew out the chain and the amulet itself.

"That's the ritual amulet of the Oni, buried with the Oni woman years ago, god knows where! Sir, what will you do?"

"Listen."

"Speaking for myself," says Morris and pulls, "that treasure might very well change my fortunes at last! Blessed be the day, my friend. May goodness be its own reward."

Momo considered. The ferryman lived under the rapid rise of his land, while commerce brought coin to every home. Ancient tradition binded this people to themselves, and their collective faith they focused on one above all. Having lost that one coincided with the collapse of commerce and the ruin of their lives. And here the amulet had returned. The old ferryman found solace and hope in the homecoming of this medallion. The good old man deserved his happiness.

The ferry nudged against the shore. Our two travellers disembarked onto the rocky coast. The monk was paid his fare, wished well to his customers, spit into the shallow water, and pushed off again, receding from Momo, his tale, and the evil plague of the Oni.

Hoki froze. A bush at their feet was shivering. Approaching cautiously to inspect the possessed shrub, Hoki crouched low, pushing his nose into the leaves. A frightful commotion burst from the small branches, flapping and flopping about in a tizzy. A paw pinned a pheasant to the ground.

"Mercy! You know not what you do! My chicks will starve or be eaten, your souls painted black with their blood, stained forever by your thoughtless actions!"

Momotaro, the giant, bent and swallowed the bird in the palm of one hand. "You will live, bird. Tell me of the Oni."

The passions of a bird are fleeting, the darkest terror fading to blank idiocy in but the blink of a sandy eye. "The Oni are an odd lot," chirps the pheasant, quite ready to converse, "with their fires and chanting, bells, flutes and headdress. Their forest forays and cleansing of the ocean waves, obeisance to the sun and worship of his sister. The latest Oni woman was quite mad. She filled my nest with her hair once. My sister swears she put eggs in her underpants. Many on the island worshipped with them. And as the island did well, so did they, all attributed to the magic of the Oni, prophecy fulfilled. I'm not so certain myself. They put on a good show. And their members shared a bond. That bond itself has great value. That bond brought about the downfall of the Oni as well. It's all a little confusing."

"You are a witness to all, bird."

"Hatched and bred on this island, as my mother before me. My first daylight coincided with the ascension of the mad queen of the Oni. The ports stocked, docked, and managed ships throughout the night at that time. The Oni were well respected under the stewardship of the mad queen's mother. Near all of the island would come to take part in the solstice events hosted by

Oni fire. A bunch of naked crazies if you ask me. Even then the officials had already seized control of most of the workings of the island. The Oni were a ritual, bonding, ceremonial celebration of culture, presiding over little more than festivals, marriages, births and deaths. The powers of the Oni were eroding by the moon. We might as well get going. Why are we just standing here? What's wrong with you, giant?"

"Bring me to the Oni."

"Alright. Walk south for a while. That's better. Fewer people would come for their rituals, the mad queen's antics wrought disrepute on the Oni. Whether or not the officials managed well their duties I do not know. I suspect they are as foolish and incompetent as most. Yet the island thrived!

Commerce and trade, culture and finance, investment and profit fell at their feet. The officials themselves were not quiet in their self appreciation. Never enough for them, the praise, and here were these loony claims of dark forces preparing the land and this people for greatness at command of the gods. Yes, through this forest and over the ridge, drop to the hollow a clearing we'll find."

An ancient land. A bare canopy reaching in beseeching prayer to the heavens. A quiet cathedral, carrying the chirp of our pheasant to the clouds and beyond.

"The officials were certainly jealous of the Oni. Moreover, Oni ritual practice could and would interfere with commerce. Shipping lanes were blocked by floating

Oni rafts, and smoke from their fires wafted into trade centres. Not to mention that wild witch and her worrisome ways! Worst of all, this large block of persons all pulled together. They could manipulate voting to their ends. So the officials made a dreadful decision, those fools. A fatal losing blow for the island."

Below in the clearing, a circle of stone. An alter, a dais, a carving of bone. A lady is lustful, if living, would moan.

"There it is. Since the hunt of the mad queen the island's social structures have disintegrated. Storms ravaged the shore. Modern transport has made stop over ports unnecessary. The various coin of neighbouring lands have stabilized in relative value, robbing the island of a very profitable enterprise. Maybe some seasonal cyclical climactic disadvantages have occurred to reduce the yield of the land. Anyhow, the people suffer. In their despair, they band together once again. An new Oni king has ascended! Here we are. Set me there, please. Yes."

The bird released with a nod and a wink, flew into the forest, forever a link in the tale of a peach boy, a much needed friend, till ears cannot hear Momotaro will not end.

OFFICIALS

Momotaro stands before the stone alter, the dog at his side. Shadows stretch as the sun sets behind the broken ridge surrounding, an amphitheatre of tribute to the gods, their gifts, and their generosity. King of the Oni Algarth emerges from the dark of his lair and approaches the alter, opposite our hero.

"Welcome, Momotaro. We rejoice at your safe arrival. The gods shine upon us this day. Would you care to restore my ancestral medallion?"

The forest dark held breath and a thick silence punished the anxious.

"No."

"Come, Momotaro. Let me offer you a drink. Come to my home. I will have food prepared for you."

"No." Deep and resonant. "I have heard your plea. I must hear others. We go to the city."

The many eyes of the woods watched. "The Oni have no desire to parade into the centres of office and trade. That would be suspicious and could provoke a security response from the officials. Momotaro, I wish you good fortune, and an open door should you want it. I hope you stay long, but please make one final visit before you depart, to return my family heirloom. Farewell."

Momo and Hoki went on their way, leaving alter and priest in the wake. Pursuing the ends of a promise, for justice and peace are at stake. Along do they journey together, through forest, by river, round lake. For honour and truth and all goodness, for virtue this path do they take.

Paths become trails become roads become stares, little does Momo care, they'd scattered, frightened, from one menacing glare. "The officials are where?", and many did point with magnetic precision towards the path our heroes did follow. Soon there were fences and fields turned to furrow, and structures and buildings, but static, unfeeling and hollow. To the courthouse our Momo is led by a lad, a kindness he wouldn't forget. The lad skipped off swiftly receding, his story untold as of yet. That lad is you, my dear reader, Momotaro and you have now met.

A courthouse, meant to awe and inspire, is large and of considerable weight. Finally a building fit for our Momo. Would he agree with the application of this justice? We hope such is possible. But corruption, abuse, and self interest are pervasive infectious disease of the spirit, metastasizing in the heart of man . And here?

Open the giant doors, and in we proceed to the halls of great justice. The preserve of our liberty, safety, and honour, blind to our religious, financial, ethnic, and sexual proclivities, and the posts most worthy of our most respectable, so greatly honoured are we at your most illustrious presence and approval my lord! my liege lay siege to your tower of illegitimate power. Our societal structure must realign on responsible resource and production management. The phantom of financial assets not backed by real world asset is a fog, a hubris, an impractical perpetual engine of growth, hastening the catastrophic collapse we force upon the future. An era must end of financial manipulation. Their every move artificially adjusts the price of all commodities of trade across all sectors immediately. Every one of them is sticking his thumb on the scales. Is Momo oblivious to all this? He is not.

Officials are as officials are, puffed up with self importance. The erosion of funding had them snapping jaws over scraps for the very necessities of life. Water, sewage, their very salaries were threatened. Fingers of an orchestral maestro at allegretto flow slow in comparison. Officials fired finger canons one to the next leaving none alive to tell the tale. Then went home to steak supper and did much the same again the next day and the next. Momo addresses the fat old one in the middle, as the fat old one on the left disgusted one by his very appearance, and the serious middle aged fellow on the right smelled of interrogative smug.

"I toiled as no man can to retrieve this medallion. It is mine. You say the Oni king has the right to this amulet?" Hoki was astonished.

"Please record for me now the following statements if you would, dear. On this, the tenth day of the tenth month, plaintiff registers a complaint with a former ruling of the court of the island of Onigashima. Here, sir, if you would, are the essential documents. Before the court can legally hear your case, we need proof of your identity. Please prepare documentation stating your name, birthplace and date, your present residence and any residence you have stayed in during the past nine years, the same for your mother and father, work histories with testimonials from previous employers, then consult your local security offices and prepare a full federal criminal background form, sealed by municipal governance, then we can talk about the paperwork to file your case of grievance and appeal."

A thunderous fist, born of the fire of the gods, slams onto the nearest table, shattering it at the knees. A deafening crash brought elbows to ear across the room. Some frightened few sought refuge beneath bureaus, by bookshelves. Momo utters not, yet the heat of his rage communicates full well the fury and consequence of Momo crossed. The fate of officials, the Oni, the island were kneeded in the fists of Momo's monstrous anger. Is Momo a monster?

Without hurry, small steps and patient looks, our great hero sees through the huddles of fleshy balding blobs. Experts in advertising their hollow worth, fortunes frittered in fraud at their fingers, outrageous narcissism rewarded, aggrandized. Media may change, but town criers live long, and the relationship between media and politic is of mutual benefit. Media then turns to commerce with her other hand, and the three skip down the golden brick road to their mansions on the coast. Others have jobs. It all works. But for whom, Momo muses. And now is a time of need.

The fabled fury of a monster erupts from within Momotaro. The anger of the gods is worthy of legend, words of a violence never survived, horrors untold for unseen, unremembered, but for the gore that must one day be cleaned. Hoki quietly and sadly sneaks out before all the bloodshed begins, unwilling to suffer the stain forever of unforgivable sin. When Momo emerges, dripping in blood, he paces for the coast, to wash, meditate, and converse with the realm of conscience few have confronted.

A cause of suffering has been alleviated for the community. These some several dozen few men sucked resources from the people of the island in taxes and fines and suffocating bureaucracy, providing little of want for the people in return. They are no more.

What will become of these people? Will the Oni bind them once again, tempting worship for peace with the gods? Let them fish and trade. Let them pursue contact with other peoples. They are well placed to succeed without the pretence to power of one kind or another. Is a leadership necessary for these people of some hundred? Do we grow into a useful leadership from some hundreds to some thousands? Do we exceed that usefulness and representativeness at some too many number?

The slaughter in the hall was sung in terror about the town, quickly reaching far afield. All hoped fisherman Wilbar would hurry along and clean those body parts out of the courthouse, and Wilgick the carpenter would bury them out of the way. Wildon could read and would know where's best for the papers and schedules and such, with Wildic by his side, but don't hope for much.

We'll muddle by, and no one will miss the officials. Their families went begging, to no purpose and starved in the streets in their shame. For none cared to carry the weight of a child, spoilt, bitter, entitled and smug, with the sweat of their efforts up the hill of time. It feels increasingly steep the higher you climb, though the berries up there are first choice.

The Oni

From the sea Momo marches, to fate's final claim for the amulet of the Oni. The Oni had accumulated after the savage sacrifice in the halls of justice. The young and the women encircled the alter, silently ecstatic their treasure returned at last. Momo approaches, with Hoki by his side.

"Hail fellow, well met! You have returned my medallion! How gracious of you Momotaro. I appre..."

"No."

A stir. A rustle. A crunch. Eyes blinking in the black of the forest, an complicated dao of emotion torments the Oni clan. Fear, for the fate of the officials was known. Hope, for the amulet has returned.

"I return to the Orchid. You may come. Correspond with the people. Return before a year. Your future is secure. The amulet is spurious temptation for you. I have earned it, I will keep it. What is earned must not be taken away. Work and you will be well." Hoki rolled over in disbelief.

Algarth the Oni king considered his prospects. Momo could not be compelled, that was certain. Stay and manage, replacing the insidious officialdom with a moderate blend of theocratic autocracy. Enticing. But being Oni still had meaning to Algarth. "I will come."

The island of Onigashima was left to fare as she would, through the winds, waves and seasons of a year, their king following faithful to the core of his ancient tradition. What of Algarth? He is no fool. He knows there is much he does not know. He believes in his experience. He has been taught that the land profits from the presence of the medallion. It is a mistake. But this belief spreads, like a virus. For many, this virus is actually beneficial. Quite pleased to be told what is what, not wanting to question established authority, which they take for evidence, they allow themselves led. Do they suffer for doing so? No. There is a bond, a kinship in the clan. A ready community, holding one's hand through the storms and tremors of life. They are well compensated.

Algarth was no fool. He knew what he didn't know, and he didn't know that the amulet brought good fortune. Yet his forefathers had done so and those before that yet again, he, Algarth would not break the great Oni tradition, centuries of their history, to his fickle and uncertain misgivings.

Invited as he was he would follow the fate of his family charm, the seed of his family tree. The people could carry on the traditions, his family spread wide with uncles and cousins, as is so in small communities of time gone by. He could be replaced by a brother, or, eventually, his daughter. Sad, though, were he not to recover the amulet.

"Momotaro, great giant, before we board this ferry. Perhaps I am hasty to commit. I, too, have home and family. You will never give me the amulet. I understand. Come back to my home. Let me crown you king of the Oni. Then you may depart with the amulet, and the good fortune of our people will be secure in you."

Momo is inscrutable. We can only guess as to limitless tides that swell beneath his surface. Perhaps he had a good opinion of Algarth. Whether his mad preachings were a paralyzing irrational poison to the people, or a salve and cure for their suffering was due much to Algarth himself, and not so to the creed and philosophy he spread. Some following him in his inheritance of this mantle may be harmful. But that may well be said of an elected, representative group. For now, under present circumstances, Algarth was, perhaps, worthy of such leadership. Perhaps Momo was happy to be crowned king of the Oni. Perhaps he was tired after his mass murder.

Momo and Algarth turned from the water, and began the walk back to the Oni lair. Hoki thinks something is wrong. Algarth walks quickly, with anxious hope, and soon they are back before the alter, to the cautious surprise of those who saw, spreading infectiously amongst the clan. More and more follow.

"I, Algarth, am Oni!" our boy proclaims, and palms rub vigorously in response. "And I will stay with the people. Our ancient medallion, that precious portal to the good will of the gods, will depart with Momotaro. The Oni will shelter beneath his enormous strength in spirit not in person, as I pronounce Momotaro King of the Oni. His good fortune will harbour our own. May the gods find affection for our great King."

Each among the men and women searched within his soul for a path forward. This new King was fearsome. The amulet would be safe under his protection. The amulet was of the Oni. Palms rubbed in appreciation. Then a mistake was made. Several enthusiastic acolytes rushed forward to Momo, and grovelled at his feet. Another shook in spasms, one more in tongues, a third in dance, and behind him chants of ooga ooga caught fire.

The thunderous fist of the gods hammered heat into the alter of stone, quaking the very earth beneath their feet. "No!", boomed stern Momo. This impressive feat encouraged the excited into a frenzy, and Momo's fury would not be restrained. A savage blaze set Momo marauding amongst the acolytes, tearing heads from bodies, crushing others under foot, hurling women and children into the forest, leagues beyond the treeline, till all scattered, screaming in horror and fear. Momo had one final sentence to the cowering Algarth. "They must not kneel!"

Whether Algarth acquiesced would distract us from the conclusion of our tale. The burst of carnage past, horrifying and bloody, Algrath the Oni, harmonizing a flat seventh to shape fate's chord forward, thought only of tomorrow for Onigashima. "Our great King will depart, carrying the soul of our people under his protection. See, now, that we are secure. May the favour the gods shine on King Momotaro reflect upon us in turn." A woman, handsome but whimpering in fear, unsteady on her feet, emerges from the Oni lair. Algarth beckons. She is his wife. Delicate and graceful in what movement she could control, yet sniffing and snivelling, as the sight of a decapitated, though familiar, body still leaking upset her. Her shaking arm offered a sack to unmoving

King Momo. "Millet dumplings. You will be hungry." Momo received the offering. And departed.

Not steps from the treeline, his home-ward journey just begun, an alarmed oof chirps as Hoki paws up a trunk, one branch up upon which sat a nest. Momo looks in on his pleasant pheasant friend. "Great Momo! Thank you for the culling. The humans were an infestation, my friend. The fowl of the island heartily approve!" Momo leaves a goodly portion of millet dumplings for the pheasant and her family. And de-parts.

Momo boards the ferry with the calm of the deepest ocean recess. The obliging monk is grateful for the fare. "You've saved me half my pocket, good sir! The financial assault of those thieving officials was beggaring the people. When I heard of your murders, I hurried along to the courthouse and dyed one of my shirts in their blood." Knudging the far shore, Momo disembarks, pays his fare, and leaves a goodly portion of millet dumplings for the monk, may he prosper. And departs.

Hoki and his loyal companion, the unfathomable giant Momotaro have a journey before them of pleasant repose into a blossoming spring of universal peace.

The End

Pardon Me...

i   Quite the racket those monks had going on. Devilishly tricky to debunk their claims. Travellers would arrive after a gruelling journey, lean and taut, some on the verge of collapse, and desperate, desperate, desperate. A little time with the monks and the travellers recover their strength for the journey home, whatever the monks have done, or claimed but not done. If the fortunes of the traveller improve in life thereafter, the monks are given their due in reputation. And, considering the desperation necessary in undertaking such a journey in the first place, their fortunes could only but improve. As an added incentive to help the monks in their success, the traveller is more than likely to claim that his journey had a profound impact on the core of his being, and, going forward, he or she has adopted the best of all principles as personal commandments, and he or she will adhere to these incorruptibly. For if the traveller were completely honest, he might say that yes, he saw the monks. And now he has returned unchanged. But then the journey was a fool's errand, and the traveller a fool for undertaking it. The public is all too ready to agree that, yes, the man has changed. The monks are all knowing. Give over your treasures to the monks. And knowing people as I do, a fair few just might.

Acknowledgments

The one and only Hugo is at the core of what I do. He is the rhyme, he is the reason, he is the impetus. The Fairie Tales don't happen if there never was a you.

You came all of a sudden on a dark mid-summer's night. Now dark has been abolished and every eve is bright. The Tales are written for you, they are your birthright.

You are written in the margins, you are here in every scene. You're the heart of every hero, you are every villain's spleen. You are the only critic I want to please with this cuisine.

Wherever life does take you, I will always take your side. Anytime there's danger I will always be your guide. Any malice, any anger, any hate you have inside, for you I will do anything, I always will abide.

Hugo, when I'm dead and gone, or when you've left the nest, there is no need for sorrow on life's merry pointless quest. Every problem can be solved, and every issue be addressed. When death comes to take me, I swear I won't protest, so long as Hugo lives on healthy, happy, I can rest.

Through trials and tribulations, Hugo, never once forget: for you alone I've lived this life and I feel no regret.

Author

Once I was child, in the garden I did play. Satisfaction I would seek and I did not delay. From game to game, from friend to friend, I sought out pleasure til the end, when mother called and home I'd go, backpack dragging, footsteps slow.

I grew much bigger day by day, and change, they did, the games I'd play. But still inside I felt the child, unruly, impatient, proud and wild. How could I attain some pearls? Then, perhaps, I'd catch the girls. I'd scheme and plan and plot and grouse to earn fate's fortune from my stool in the alehouse.

Older still I soon became, by then I'd given up the game of chasing fortune here and there, while tearing daily at my hair. Let her do as she will please, I'll not go begging on my knees. I'll lock myself in tower keep, and for a while I'd moan and weep, for fortune was beyond my reach, she lives in walls I cannot breech.

Finally, when quite alone, a soul all withered, a heart of stone, I sat down sadly at my desk and began to write this picaresque. Satisfaction did it bring when quite alone to boldly sing and let my inner voice be heard. A sound there comes from a once silent bird.

Who did hear my lonely call? Who did watch as I did scrawl? To my feet fate thought to crawl.

Hell's Press

In a prison does a man reside, a shell, a mortal coil. Live, he does, if one did ask, a life of constant toil. Plead, he will, when times are tough, in Hell too soon to boil. Meet, he must, before he does, the Liars only Foyle. Annointed will he be that day with Heaven's sacred oil. Hell's grand feast for when he comes is all too sure to spoil.

Printed in the USA
CPSIA information can be obtained
at www.ICGtesting.com
JSHW081728081123
51651JS00004B/137

9 781738 132140